RED CARD
FOR THE REF

Alan Durant got the football bug at the age of eight and has never looked back. He supports Manchester United and his favourite player of all time is George Best. Among his many books for children are *Creepe Hall, Return to Creepe Hall, Jake's Magic, Spider McDrew, Happy Birthday, Spider McDrew, The Fantastic Football Fun Book* and the picture books *Big Fish Little Fish* and *Angus Rides the Goods Train*. He also writes novels and mystery stories for older children. Alan lives just south of London with his wife, three young children, cat and a garden shed in which he does all his writing. He hopes one day to be able to fully understand the offside rule.

Titles in the **Leggs United** series

All **Leggs United** titles can be ordered at your local bookshop or are available by post from Book Service by Post (tel: 01624 675137).

RED CARD
FOR THE REF

ALAN DURANT

ILLUSTRATED BY
CHRIS SMEDLEY

MACMILLAN CHILDREN'S BOOKS

First published 1998 by Macmillan Children's Books
a division of Macmillan Publishers Limited
25 Eccleston Place, London SW1W 9NF
Basingstoke and Oxford
www.macmillan.co.uk
Associated companies throughout the world

ISBN 0 330 35130 3

3 5 7 9 8 6 4 2

A CIP catalogue record for this book is available from
the British Library.

Typeset by SX Composing DTP, Rayleigh, Essex
Printed and bound in Great Britain by Mackays of Chatham plc, Kent

LEGGS UNITED
FAMILY TREE

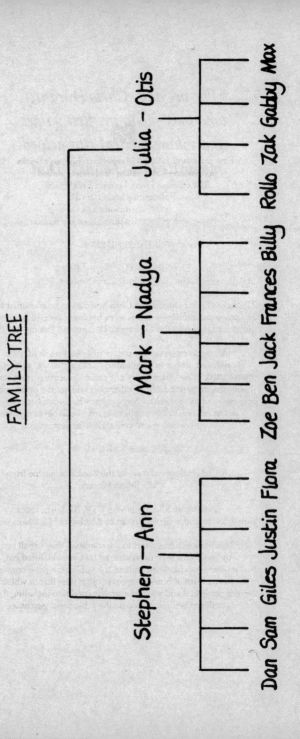

Stephen – Ann

Dan Sam Giles Justin Flora

Mark – Nadya

Zoe Ben Jack Frances Billy

Julia – Otis

Rollo Zak Gabby Max

For my dad, Chris Durant,
who took me to my first games
and whose tactical tips helped
me write this. Thanks, Dad!

Chapter One
WHAT A DUMP!

"**A**aah!" Dan Legg stumbled backwards across the rough wooden floor, tripped over a sports bag and tumbled to the ground. Luckily, he landed on his bottom, so no harm was done – except to his pride. He sat for a moment where he had fallen, grimacing. Around him the room was noisy with laughter.

"Hey, Dan," chirped his younger sister Sam, "could you do that again? I only saw the last bit."

"Ha, ha, very funny," Dan said grouchily, getting to his feet. He looked accusingly at the broken wall hook that had caused his tumble. All he'd done was pull on it a little as he hung up his

1

clothes and the hook had come away in his hand. "This changing room's an old dump," he grumbled. "It must be even more ancient than Archie."

Archie was Archibald Legg, the manager of Leggs United, a junior football team formed from the children of three related families. He was also a ghost, having died over sixty years before in a freak accident, struck down by lightning while playing for the local football team, Muddington Rovers. Right now he was resting inside the old ball that he had haunted since his death.

"Talking of Archie," said Zak Browne, Dan's cousin and best friend. "Isn't it about time we called him?" Archie always gave his team a talk before they started a match. This afternoon Leggs United were playing at Old Malden, one of the weakest teams in the Muddington District Junior League, and the kick-off was less than twenty minutes away.

Sam Legg picked up the old brown leather football from one of the creaky wooden benches. She started to rub it gently, while wailing, "Arise, O Archie. Archie, arise!" She spoke in a funny quavery voice that at one time had made the rest of the team giggle. But they were used to it now.

What happened next, though, was quite unexpected.

There was a kind of fizzing and flickering as there usually was before Archie appeared. But it was followed by an astonishing explosion as Archie whooshed out of the ball so vigorously he hit the ceiling!

His young relations stared at him, goggle-eyed.

"Wow!" said Sam, when Archie had come down to earth again. "That was amazing."

Archie glowed as though he were on fire. His

red hair stood up on end like a shock of flames. His bushy eyebrows twitched like electrified caterpillars. His huge walrus moustache quivered at the tips. There was an odd ruddiness to his usually pale face.

"Are you OK, Archie?" Dan asked tentatively.

"OK?" Archie queried briskly. "OK? Why, I have never felt better in my life – I mean, my death. I think there must be an electricity power station somewhere nearby." Archie had discovered that electricity gave him energy. He would often charge up on household appliances, such as Dan's mum's sewing machine or the television. This afternoon, though, he was clearly already fully charged.

He looked about him, taking in the shabby changing hut. The children expected him to be critical, but he wasn't. "Hmm, seems a pleasant enough place," he remarked lightly, resting one foot on the old football.

"Pleasant!" Dan exclaimed. "It's awful. It's all damp and rotten and the paint's coming off the walls. It must be about a hundred years old."

Archie bristled with outrage. "Poppycock!" he proclaimed. "It's a fine building. It's got

4

character. Who knows what great players may have changed within these four walls down the years." His expression went a little dreamy.

"I bet Herbert Chapman wouldn't have approved," Dan humphed. Herbert Chapman had been the manager of Arsenal during the 1930s and his team had been the best in the land. Whenever Archie spoke of Chapman or his players, it was always with the greatest admiration.

"Ah, laddy, how wrong you are," Archie declared with a dismissive waggle of his moustache. "Herbert Chapman may have ended up at the marble halls of Highbury, but he started life in far more humble surroundings. He was the son of a miner, you know, and he played for such lowly teams as Stalybridge Rovers, Sheppey United and Worksop." Archie smiled. "Like all true geniuses," he intoned smugly, "Herbert Chapman was at home wherever he found himself."

"Well, I bet he never found himself bumping on his bottom on a splintery wooden floor like I just did," Dan muttered darkly, tugging at one ear.

Archie gave his captain a withering look. "I should think not," he retorted. "Bumping along on one's bottom is for babies, not grown men."

Once again, the hut echoed with laughter. Giles and Justin, Dan's younger twin brothers, collapsed in a hooting heap on the floor. Dan's face flushed red.

"I wasn't bumping along!" he protested indignantly. "I–"

But his explanation got no further. It was brought to a sudden halt by a loud *rat-a-tat-tat* on the changing-room door.

Chapter Two
MEETING THE REF

The door whined open and a tubby man peered in. "Ah, hello there," he said, smiling. "My name's Keith Dixon. I'm the referee."

The Leggs United players regarded the stranger with interest. He was dressed in a black kit with a watch on each wrist and a whistle round his neck, but somehow he didn't really *look* like a ref, Dan thought.

For a start, the kit he wore didn't seem to fit him properly. The shirt was baggy at the top, but stretched to bursting round his big beer belly. The shorts hung down almost to his knees, rather like Archie's. He looked about the same age as Stephen Legg, Dan's dad, but he didn't look half as fit. His face was very chubby and speckled with stubble, and his black, shiny hair was slicked flat against his scalp. He had about five chins.

Archie was clearly unimpressed. He glared at the ref with scorching disdain and tutted.

"I just thought I'd come in and, er, introduce myself," the referee continued. His pasty face bore a broad, easy smile, while his small eyes glanced busily round the room. His gaze alighted finally on the old ball.

"That's an interesting football you have there," he said amiably. "You don't see many like that these days."

Dan nodded. "It belonged to an old relative of ours, who used to be a footballer," he explained, picking the ball up. He looked at Archie, who raised one questioning eyebrow. "A very good footballer," he added quickly. Archie waggled his moustache and beamed.

"Oh, I see, a family heirloom, eh?" said the ref and he rubbed his hands together. "Probably worth a bob or two I shouldn't wonder."

"Oh, we don't care about that!" Sam snorted with a toss of her head.

"No," Dan agreed. "We'd never sell it. It's, er . . ." He hesitated, struggling for the right word.

"It's special," said Zak, coming to his friend's assistance.

"Well, I'm sure it is," said the ref. "You want to take good care of that. It's probably an antique."

"Eh?" Dan queried.

"He means it's very old and valuable," said Zak, who often watched *Antiques Roadshow* with his mum, Julia Browne. It was her favourite TV programme.

"Yeah, like you, Archie," quipped Sam and the others laughed.

The ref looked bewildered. "Who's this Archie, then?" he asked with a puzzled frown. He was actually staring straight at Archie – but he couldn't see him, for the phantom manager was invisible to everyone except his family.

"Archibald Legg to you, Mr Referee," boomed Archie, drawing himself up to his full height. But his words were in vain because the referee couldn't hear him either.

"Archie's our manager!" cried Giles.

"He's a ghost!" shouted Justin. Then, as one, they raised their arms in the air and made spooky whoo-whooing noises.

The referee smiled. "Oh, I see. It's a game, is it?" he said with a knowing nod that made his many chins wobble. He put his hands on his hips and stared at Archie, as if he really could see him. Then, in a loud, slow voice, he said, "Well, Archie, I'd better let you get on with your team talk, hadn't I?" He turned away momentarily and winked at the twins. "But no frightening the other team, mind," he went on, "or I'll have to show you the red card." He drew a red card from his top pocket and waved it in Archie's direction. Then, laughing heartily at his joke, he walked out.

Archie was not amused. "Red card indeed," he sniffed. "In my day, referees just pointed their finger and told you to go. There was none of this red card nonsense." He flapped one pale hand dismissively.

"Did *you* ever get sent off, Archie?" asked Dan.

"Certainly not!" Archie bristled. "Why, laddy, I was never even booked. Foul play, as you know, is something I deplore."

"What about arguing with the ref?" Sam enquired slyly. Archie often shouted abuse at referees during matches and once or twice he'd even run on to the field and tried to grab hold of them.

"Yes, well, er," Archie blustered. His moustache twitched uneasily. "The referee's decision is final, of course," he stated firmly. "Players should never dispute it."

"What about managers?" said Zak with a conspiratorial glance at Sam.

"Ah, now that's quite another matter," Archie replied loftily. "Managers can dispute all they like."

"Especially when the ref can't hear them," Dan suggested.

"And if they're geniuses," Sam added with mock-seriousness. Archie was always telling the children what a genius he was.

Archie ignored Sam's teasing tone and took her remark as a compliment. "Precisely," he declared with a contented smile. "This afternoon, however, I shall be a paragon of

virtue: not a word of dissent shall pass my lips. I shall take every refereeing decision with the patience and grace of a saint." As he spoke these words, a saintly halo did indeed glimmer above his head. "Now, enough about referees," he said gravely. "It is time to talk about this afternoon's match . . ."

Chapter Three
WEIRD DECISIONS

Old Malden were a struggling team. They'd lost a few players since the start of the season, their captain Ash told Dan, and they were finding it hard to put out a full team.

"We'd only have had ten players today if Harvey hadn't turned up this morning and asked to join us," Ash said. He nodded at a tall, blond-haired boy who was doing keep-ups with casual skill.

"He looks really good," said Dan admiringly.

"I hope so," said Ash. He pulled a wry expression. "The rest of us aren't."

At that moment, the ref arrived. He was

puffing hard and he'd only come from the changing hut. Dan wondered what he'd be like when the game got going.

"Right," the ref wheezed. "Ready to start?" Dan and Ash both nodded. "OK, then, get your teams in position," the ref ordered and he blew his whistle.

The two captains gave the referee a questioning stare. "Aren't you going to toss a coin to see who kicks off?" Dan said with a small tug of his ear.

"Oh, yes, of course," the ref mumbled. He fumbled in his pockets for a moment or two, then, "Has anyone got a coin?" he asked sheepishly.

"My dad'll have one," Dan offered. He went over to Stephen Legg, who was standing on the touchline with his brother Mark and Zak's dad Otis Browne. Seconds later, he returned with a shiny pound coin.

"Well done, son," said the ref. He tossed the coin and Dan called, "Heads."

"Sorry, tails," said the ref and he slipped the coin into the pocket of his shorts. Then he blew his whistle again for the match to kick off.

Leggs United started well. In their very first attack, Sam put Zak in on goal and his shot went narrowly wide. Moments later, Sam herself shot against the post. But Old Malden's luck couldn't hold. A long kick upfield from defence by Dan found Zak in space once more. Controlling the ball immediately, he skipped past one defender and then a second before lashing the ball into the top corner of the net. One–nil to Leggs United.

The first half was all Leggs. Zak scored a second goal and the wingers, Ben and Frances (two of the Leggs United triplets), scored one apiece. They each celebrated by doing a cartwheel that they'd been practising. But neither had got it quite right yet. Ben's turned into a somersault and Frances ended up tangling her legs and falling flat on her face.

Old Malden, meanwhile, hardly had a single attack. Harvey was their most skilful player, but he seemed to be more interested in doing tricks than playing proper football. When the ball came to him, he flicked it from foot to foot or knee to knee. He tried dragbacks and backheels, but he never ran with the ball once. In fact, he didn't seem that bothered about the game.

But Harvey's performance wasn't half as odd as the referee's. He seemed to be a little confused about what sport the teams were playing. When the ball went off for a throw-in, he blew his whistle and called for a "line-out". And when an Old Malden player committed a clear handball, he waved *play on*.

The weirdest incident came near the end of the half when Gabby, the Leggs United goalie, threw the ball to Dan and the ref peeped his whistle again. This time he shouted, "Scrum!"

"Scrum?" Dan queried.

"Yes, that was a forward pass," said the ref a little breathlessly.

"But this is football, not rugby!" Dan exclaimed. "The goalie's allowed to throw the ball forward."

The referee gaped at Dan, his large mouth opening and shutting like a goldfish's. "Oh, did I say forward pass?" he spluttered at last. "I meant offside. The forwards were offside. Penalty to you, son."

Dan shook his head. "You mean free-kick, don't you?" he suggested.

"Free-kick, yes," the ref confirmed testily. "Now hurry up and take it or I'll have to show you a yellow card for time-wasting."

"But . . ." Dan protested. Then he remembered what Archie had said before the game about not arguing with the ref. "OK," he sighed.

The referee's decisions got even more bizarre in the second half. Instead of goal kicks he called for "drop-outs" and twice when the ball was headed forward he blew his whistle and said it was a "knock-on". On the touchline, Archie's saintly halo turned into a fireball. He blazed with outrage, yet somehow he managed to restrain himself from shouting at the ref.

The ref's strangest decision of all came about fifteen minutes from the end, when he showed Harvey the red card . . . for doing nothing at all! Some of the Old Malden players ran over to protest, but Harvey didn't seem to care. He trotted away without a word.

Leggs United won the game easily. The final score was 6–0, Zak and Sam scoring second-half goals. But the talk at the end of the game was about the ref, not the result.

"That ref was terrible," Dan said to Ash when they shook hands afterwards.

"Yeah, he was a joke," Ash agreed. "I don't know why he sent off Harvey."

"No, nor do I," said Dan incredulously. "I don't think he knows the rules."

"He told us it was one of his first games in the League," Ash replied. "I think it should be his last . . ."

The captains' poor opinion of the referee was mild, though, compared to Archie's displeasure. Back in the changing room, he could no longer contain his rage at the official's incompetence.

"Simpleton, ass, blithering nincompoop!" he stormed. "The man should be locked up in a mental asylum. I've never seen such an abominable display of refereeing." A flaming aura pulsed around the irate phantom. "*He* is the one who should have been shown the red card!" he raved.

"I thought you said you weren't going to dispute the ref's decisions," said Sam cheekily, wrinkling her freckly nose.

Archie glowered at his young relative and disappeared abruptly into the old football. There was a sudden urgent cry from the changing room next door.

"Hey!" cried a boy's distressed voice. "My watch! Someone's taken my watch!"

Chapter Four
QUALITY GOODS

Ash, the Old Malden captain, was in a real state. It was he who'd called out and *his* watch that had been taken. In fact, it was even worse than that, for the watch actually belonged to his dad, as he told the Leggs United team tearfully when they went to see what all the noise was about. The watch was a Rolex and very expensive – Ash had brought it to the game to impress his friends. But he'd borrowed it without asking his dad, and now it was gone. Money had been stolen from the home team's changing room too. Fortunately for the Leggs, they hadn't had anything of value with them – except the old football, of course, and that had been out on the touchline.

The thief had obviously gone into the changing room while the game was on. Harvey reckoned he saw him. There was a man around the back of the hut, he said, when he was walking back there after getting sent off.

"Did you see what he looked like?" Dan asked.

Harvey frowned thoughtfully. "He was tall," he said slowly, "with, er, ginger hair. Yeah, long, curly ginger hair – and a hat."

"What kind of hat?" Dan wondered, trying to draw a picture in his head of the suspected thief.

"Er, well, it was a big hat," said Harvey. "With stripes on it, like, er, like a leopard."

"A leopard?" Sam queried. "Leopards don't have stripes. They have spots."

"Yeah, that's what I meant, spots," Harvey agreed.

"Well, he should be easy to find," Dan said positively. Then he turned toward his team-mates. "Did anyone else see him?" he asked. But no one could recall having seen anyone that afternoon who fitted Harvey's description.

Everyone felt very sorry for Ash – Dan in

particular. He'd once been responsible for losing the old football that housed Archie and he remembered how awful he'd felt. For a while he'd been sure that the old ball was lost for ever – and Archie with it.

He looked at the ball now, held snugly under his arm. Archie was still inside, presumably recovering from his efforts to control himself during the match. Dan thought again how lucky he'd been that the ball hadn't been stolen, just misplaced temporarily. Poor Ash had no such luck.

"I wish there was something we could do to help," Dan said to Sam and Zak, as they went off towards the refreshments van where their parents were having a cup of tea.

"Yeah," Zak nodded, his black ringlets swaying in front of his face.

"I'd like to catch that dirty thief!" hissed Sam fiercely. Then, "Oof!" she exclaimed, as she bumped straight into the referee, who was just walking out from his little room at the end of the changing hut. Sam bounced off the referee's huge stomach and fell back into Dan. For the second time that afternoon, Dan found himself sitting on his bottom on the ground.

It was the ref, though, who appeared to come off worst. He bent over wheezing as if he'd had all the breath knocked out of him.

"Are you all right?" asked Zak, who was the only one who hadn't been bumped.

The referee waved one podgy hand, as if to say he was OK, but it was several moments before he stopped gasping enough to be able to speak.

"Hoo, you winded me there all right, sonny," he said to Sam. "You must be made of iron." Usually Sam got cross if anyone called her a boy. But she didn't this time, because she was rather pleased at the referee's remark. It made her sound really tough, she thought.

"I'm sorry," she said with unusual humility. "I wasn't looking where I was going."

"You should show her the red card," Dan quipped, now back on his feet again.

"Yes," the referee laughed a little uncomfortably. He looked down at his bag. "I wonder if one of you lads would do me a favour and carry my bag to the car," he breathed hoarsely. "It's only just over there." He pointed to an old, white and very dirty Ford Escort in the car park. On the side, someone had written *Please wash me*, with their finger.

"I'll take it," said Sam quickly, eager to show that she was strong as well as tough.

She picked up the ref's bag – and promptly dropped it again!

"Wow! That's heavy!" she declared in amazement.

"Yes, well, we refs have to carry a lot of equipment," the ref remarked airily.

"What sort of things?" Dan asked with interest. The three children gazed at the ref with expectation.

"Oh, all sorts of things," the ref replied vaguely. "Er, spare whistles, notebooks, first-aid gear, crowbars . . ."

"Crowbars?" Dan queried.

"I mean, er, chocolate bars," the ref hastily corrected himself. "You know, for energy."

"Some footballers eat bananas for energy," said Zak, who was the Leggs United expert on football facts, figures and general information.

"Tommy Banks eats bananas," Sam sighed. Tommy Banks was Muddington Rovers' star player and Sam's hero.

"Yeah, so do monkeys," teased Dan, and Sam gave him a waspish glare.

In the end, Sam and Zak each took a handle of the ref's bag and carried it between them. Dan followed behind.

"Thanks, lads," the ref muttered when they reached his car. He put his hand in his pocket and pulled out his keys. "Now, I've got this feeling you're fans of Muddington Rovers. Am I right?" he asked with an amiable smile.

The three children nodded. "Yeah," they confirmed.

"Well, I've got something in here that just might interest you," said the ref, turning the key in the lock of his car boot. He lifted the boot lid.

"Wow!" Sam cried.

"Cool," uttered Zak.

"Yeah," Dan agreed.

The boot was full of football gear. There were team strips, tracksuits, boots, trainers, shin-pads – all brand new. It was a real treasure chest.

"I've got a mate who runs a sports shop," the ref explained. "I help him out by selling stuff for him. Good stuff, mind, no rubbish. And cheap too."

The ref took out a child-sized Muddington

Rovers shirt and held it up in front of him. It looked very small against his huge stomach. "I reckon this would fit you," he said to Sam.

Sam eyed the shirt eagerly. "How much is it?" she enquired.

"Well, I usually charge £15 for a shirt like that," the ref answered, rubbing his hand over his stubbly jaw. "But seeing as you carried my bag, you can have it for £10."

"£10!" Sam exclaimed happily. £10 was a lot of money, but most football shirts, she knew, cost over three times that much.

"But, Sam, you've already got a Muddington Rovers shirt," Dan pointed out.

"Yeah, I know," said Sam, wrinkling her nose. "But it's being washed."

Dan shook his head. "You're crazy," he laughed. "Dad won't buy you a new football shirt, just because your other one's dirty."

Sam glowered at her brother, but before she could retort, Zak said, "Look, the police are here." He nodded his head towards the park entrance, through which a police car had just driven. Keith Dixon slammed down the lid of his boot.

"I'll tell you what, lads, have a think about the shirt and stuff, OK?" he said, his eyes on the approaching police car. "I'll give you my card and, if you want something, you can give me a call." He pulled out a small white card and handed it to Sam. *Keith Dixon*, it read, *Qualified Referee and Vendor of Quality Sports Goods*. Then there was a telephone number. "Now, I suppose we'd better help the police with their inquiries, eh?" he breathed and he shepherded the children away from his car and back towards the changing rooms.

Chapter Five
LOCK UP
THE REF

"Danny Bright, Bright, Bright!
Got in a fight, fight, fight!
In the night, night, night!"

When Dan returned home from school on
Monday afternoon he was treated to a noisy
rendition of the twins' new football chorus.
Danny Bright was a defender for Muddington
Rovers who had been sent off at the weekend for
fighting with an opponent.

"What do you think?" asked Giles
breathlessly.

"It's good, isn't it?" enthused Justin.

"Well . . ." Dan muttered, trying to think of a response to the awful din he'd just been subjected to. "It rhymes."

"Of course it does!" squealed Giles.

"It's a song!" Justin declared.

Then they rushed away towards the kitchen to try out the new composition on their mum, Ann Legg.

Dan watched them go with a shake of his head. His eyes caught sight of the card that the ref had given Sam, lying on the hall table. He picked it up and looked at it. Then he shook his head again. *Keith Dixon, Qualified Referee*, he read. Well, that didn't make sense, did it? To be qualified you'd have to pass a test, wouldn't you, like his mum had when she'd learned to drive? How could Keith Dixon have passed a football test when he didn't even know the rules? Some of those decisions he'd made on Saturday were completely crazy.

Still holding the card, he went into the sitting room, thinking maybe he'd call up Archie to ask him what he thought – and was surprised to see the phantom manager already there. He was hovering by the table above the old ball, glowing with contentment. Sam was there too. She was sitting at the table with a pen in her hand and a notebook open in front of her.

"What's going on?" Dan asked, intrigued.

Sam turned and gave Dan a freckly grin. "Archie's helping me with my homework," she told him. "We've got to do a project on a famous person from the twentieth century and I chose Herbert Chapman."

"An excellent decision," Archie nodded approvingly. He wrinkled his moustache in a superior manner. "At least you'll learn one useful thing at school," he remarked drily.

Dan humphed. Typical Sam, he thought. He knew she'd only chosen Herbert Chapman because it meant she wouldn't have to do much work – she could get Archie to do it for her!

Mention of the great Arsenal manager, however, gave Dan the opening he wanted to talk about his own subject of interest.

"I wonder what Herbert Chapman would have said about that ref on Saturday," he mused.

Archie snorted. His eyebrows hopped and jiggled like frisky caterpillars. "Herbert Chapman did not suffer fools gladly," he stated gravely. "He probably would have asked to have that referee struck off immediately." He raised one bushy eyebrow. "Though, of course, we had to endure some appalling referees in our day too," he admitted.

Archie went on to tell Dan and Sam about a particularly dreadful referee called Mr Harper. He refereed the FA Cup Final of 1932 and allowed Newcastle a goal against Arsenal that should never have been given. The ball had already crossed the Arsenal dead-ball line, when the Newcastle forward kicked it. The Arsenal defenders stood still, waiting for the ref's whistle for a goal kick. But Jack Allen of Newcastle stepped in and put the ball into the net. To everyone's amazement, the referee blew for a goal! Arsenal never recovered and Newcastle went on to win the match.

The referee refused to accept that he'd made a mistake, even though the photographs proved it. He said he was only eight yards from the ball and could see clearly, but the evidence showed he was twenty-five yards away!

"Not only was he a fool, he was a liar," Archie seethed. The incident may have happened well over half a century before, but evidently it still enraged the old footballer.

"Herbert Chapman must have gone mad," Dan suggested.

"No," Archie pronounced with a sombre wag of his large head. "Herbert Chapman was a great man and like all great men he had dignity. 'The referee has made his decision and that's the end of it,' was his dignified response." Archie's eyes flared once more. "Personally I think the referee should have been locked up in the Tower of London and never released," he remarked bitterly.

Dan laughed. "That would be a bit cruel, Archie," he commented lightly. "After all, it was only a game."

Archie shimmered and glowed as if he'd been deeply affronted. "Only a game!" he exploded. "Only a game! Why, the Cup Final is the greatest event in the world." His stare challenged Dan to disagree.

"Ah, yes, of course," Dan mumbled, tugging at one ear. "What I meant was . . . well, the referee hadn't broken the law, had he? He wasn't a criminal, he just wasn't very good."

Archie drew himself up to his full height, his eyebrows meeting in a shaggy mass of red. "In my book, laddy," he retorted sharply, "that *is* a crime . . ."

"No, it's not," Sam scoffed, flicking back her fringe. "A crime's like when you steal someone's money or watch or something – like on Saturday."

"Yes," Dan affirmed. Then he told his phantom relative about the dramatic events that had occurred on Saturday after he'd retired to his old football. And Sam chipped in about the ref and his sports gear.

Archie's eyes narrowed to two flickering sparks. "Hmm," he growled. "I wouldn't trust that referee as far as I could throw him!"

It was a serious remark, but Dan and Sam laughed. The idea of Archie throwing roly-poly Keith Dixon conjured an extraordinary picture in their heads.

"How could you possibly trust a man who made so many appalling errors?" Archie continued with a fierce glare that quickly wiped the smiles from the children's faces.

"Oh yes, I agree," said Dan emphatically. "I didn't trust him either."

Sam tossed her head dismissively. "Just because he didn't offer *you* a shirt," she said pointedly. "Now, if you don't mind, I'd like to get back to my project . . ."

Chapter Six
HERBERT CHAPMAN

Over the next few days, Sam spent a lot of time talking with Archie about Herbert Chapman. Sometimes Dan and Zak sat in and listened – though they weren't allowed to speak or ask questions.

"It's my project," Sam asserted. "I'll ask the questions."

As it happened, however, Sam hardly got to speak either. Archie loved to address an audience and once he began talking, it was difficult to stop him. Sam's hand ached from trying to write down everything he told her.

Archie began with Herbert Chapman's

36

humble background. He was born in 1878 in a small village in South Yorkshire, the son of a miner, who could neither read nor write. He didn't follow his father down the pit, though; he worked as a mining engineer. At the same time, he played football for many different clubs, including Stalybridge Rovers, Grimsby, Swindon, Sheffield United and, finally, Spurs.

"And he played in yellow boots like me," said Dan, referring to the prized boots he'd won – with Archie's help – in a spot-the-ball competition.

"Precisely," said Archie.

Sam coughed impatiently and shot her brother a sharp glare. "Shh," she hissed fiercely.

"Sorry," Dan muttered in a not-at-all-sorry voice.

"Carry on, Archie," Sam commanded.

Archie went on to tell his young listeners about Herbert Chapman's great managerial career, which began at lowly Northampton and ended so gloriously at Arsenal. In between there was a period at Leeds City, who won virtually every competition during the First World War years, but were then expelled from the League for making illegal payments to players. Of course, Archie stressed, the manager himself was completely innocent.

"He wasn't a criminal, then," Dan joked – and was immediately told off by both Archie and Sam.

"Shh! Stop interrupting," Sam hissed crossly.

"Herbert Chapman, a criminal!" Archie bristled. "What a suggestion. He was the greatest man of his time. Indeed, it was said by many that he ought to have been prime minister."

"Yes," Dan agreed eagerly, "then he could have

made it a law that Arsenal always had to win!"

Dan laughed. Sam smiled pityingly and shook her head. But Archie was not amused. His eyes fizzed with contempt.

"He would certainly have done no such thing," he pronounced sharply. "Arsenal were the best team. They had no need of such knavish shenanigans."

"It was only a joke, Archie," said Dan meekly.

"Well, keep your stupid jokes to yourself," Sam instructed, her smile completely gone now. "This is a serious interview." She turned to her phantom relative with an encouraging nod. "Carry on, please, Archie," she requested with exaggerated politeness. "*I'm* listening."

Placated, Archie continued the Herbert Chapman story with his next managerial stop, Huddersfield Town. Here, as the children knew already, the famous manager won two league championships in a row before being appointed manager of Arsenal.

At the mention of Arsenal, Archie paused, his face beaming blissfully. "And that," he uttered with hushed reverence, "is where his genius truly flowered."

"Yes . . .?" Sam prompted, her pen poised above the notepad, waiting for Archie to go on. But Archie didn't go on. Instead, he looked challengingly at Sam.

"Now, lassy," he said, "I think it's time *you* did some work, don't you?"

"Eh?" Sam queried.

"You surely don't expect me to do *all* your work for you," Archie contended with a waggle of his walrus moustache. "That would be like me playing your matches for you in addition to being your manager."

Dan grinned. Clever old Archie, he thought. He was wise to Sam's game. He knew what she was up to.

"But you *know* about Herbert Chapman," Sam protested. "I don't."

"You can read, can't you?" Archie retorted. "In my day, if we wanted to find out about something, we went to our local library. It is called research." He gave Sam a steely glare. "You do have a local library, don't you?"

"Well, yes," said Sam, "but . . ."

"Then I suggest you go there," Archie interrupted brusquely. "We shall talk again when you return." He yawned theatrically. "Now, I think I deserve a rest." And with that, he quickly faded, vanishing into the old ball like dust into a vacuum cleaner.

Sam scowled at the ball as if she'd like to give it a good kick.

"It's not fair," she grumbled.

"Of course it is," Dan argued. "Archie's given you lots of help, now you've got to do some work for yourself."

"Hmph," Sam replied grumpily, as if she'd like to give Dan a kick too.

"Cheer up," Dan urged. "I'll go to the library with you, if you like. I'll see if Zak wants to come too."

This suggestion seemed to appease Sam. The frown slipped from her face and she nodded. "OK," she said softly. Her lips turned up in a half smile. "But don't forget," she pointed out, "it's *my* project."

Chapter Seven
SAM GETS BOOKED

On Saturday morning, Sam, Dan and Zak cycled to the library. They got there quite early, so it wasn't busy. In fact, there were only a couple of other customers – two old men, who'd come to read the newspapers. Well, one of them was reading. The other one had already fallen asleep with a newspaper on his lap.

"He should have stayed at home in bed," Sam remarked.

"Maybe he's been here all night," Dan suggested.

"No, he wouldn't be allowed to do that," said

Zak seriously. "Unless he's one of the librarians, I suppose."

There was a loud cough from the library desk behind them. They turned round to see a tall, elderly woman with pink-framed glasses and bluey-grey hair.

"Can I help you children?" she asked pleasantly.

The children stared at her blankly for a moment or two.

"We're looking for information about a man called Herbert Chapman," said Sam at last. "He was the manager of Arsenal."

"That's a football team," Dan added helpfully.

"Yes, I know who Arsenal are," the woman replied with a small laugh. "And I know who Herbert Chapman is, too." She gazed over her glasses at the children. "I could tell you something very interesting about Herbert Chapman," she said intriguingly.

"Oh, yes, please," Sam urged. The children stared at the librarian with eager expectation.

"Well," she said, "it was Herbert Chapman who was responsible for Gillespie Road underground station changing its name to

Arsenal." She smiled with great satisfaction.

. "Oh," said Sam, struggling to contain her disappointment. She wanted facts about football, not trains.

"Anyway," the librarian continued, "if you want to find out more, I suggest you look him up on the computer." She waved her hand vaguely at a monitor by the first set of bookshelves. Then she raised a finger. "But please remember this is a library," she instructed. "Don't disturb the other customers."

As she turned away, the three children looked at one another in puzzlement. There weren't any other customers apart from the two old men – and they were now both fast asleep!

Sam sat down at the computer terminal and typed in the words Herbert Chapman. *No match* was the message the screen flashed back at her. It offered three alternative suggestions: *Herbie the Hippo*; *Herbs and Spices, A User's Guide*; and *Herbert Finkelbottom Investigates Rocks.*

"Try just typing *Chapman*," Zak proposed.

"OK," Sam agreed. She tapped the letters out on the keyboard and hit the return key.

Now there was a whole list of suggestions –

over a hundred, in fact. Sam scrolled through them all. There were Chapmans with many different first names, but there was no mention of Herbert Chapman.

"This is hopeless," she sighed. "I'll just have to tell Archie I couldn't find anything."

"You can't do that," said Dan, tugging at his ear. "He'll be really upset if you tell him the library's got nothing on his hero."

"Well, what am I supposed to do, then?" Sam complained. "Make something up?"

Dan shook his head. "No, that wouldn't work," he said. "Archie would know. He knows everything about Herbert Chapman."

"Yeah," Zak agreed. The children stared glumly at the screen. "You could try some of the players' names," Zak suggested eventually.

"Yeah, Alex James. Type in Alex James," Dan urged.

This time, to the children's delight, there was a match. The library had a biography of the Arsenal playmaker. Sam leapt off her chair and raced away to get it.

It was quite a thick book, but a lot of it was about James's life before he joined Arsenal and his playing days after Herbert Chapman died. But there were a few chapters that featured the great manager.

The snag was that the book was in the adult section and Sam couldn't take it out on her children's ticket.

"Oh, please," Sam pleaded. "I'll look after it, I promise."

But the librarian sighed and shook her head.

"I'm sorry," she said regretfully. "Those are the rules. You'll have to read it here."

They took the book into the children's library and sat down at one of the study tables. Dan looked at his watch. "You'd better read it fast," he said. "It's not that long till lunchtime. And I want to have a kick-about before the match." That afternoon, Leggs United were playing at their home ground, The Meadow, against Belmont Bees, one of the top teams in the Muddington District Junior League.

"It's OK," said Sam airily. "I'm a fast reader."

While Sam settled down to read her book on Alex James, Dan and Zak went to choose some books to borrow. They took their time choosing, but when they returned with their books stamped, Sam still had one chapter to read.

"I'm going to look at the newspapers," Dan said, "and see if there's any football news."

"Yeah, me too," said Zak, who loved reading about football.

The old men were still asleep in their chairs, snoring gently. The newspapers they were reading had slipped to the floor in front of them. Dan bent down and started to tidy them up. As he did so, a headline on one of the pages caught his eye. *Sports Warehouse Raided!* he read. He stood up, studying the page more closely. It was

from one of the local papers that covered Muddington and other towns nearby.

The article reported a break-in at a warehouse of sports goods. Many high-quality items – including football strips, boots and balls – had been stolen. Apparently, this was the second such raid in the area during the last month. As yet, police had no leads, the paper said.

As he read, Dan had a funny tickly feeling, as if a small insect was crawling around inside him. He couldn't help thinking about Keith Dixon and his car boot full of brand new football gear. What was it he called himself? *Vendor of Quality Sports Goods*, that was it. Dan had looked up vendor in the dictionary and it meant seller. Keith Dixon sold sports stuff. But what, Dan pondered suddenly, if he stole it too? What if he really was a criminal? For some instants, his heart thumped with excitement, as he imagined himself solving a major crime. But then he pictured the podgy ref, with his pot belly and his wobbly chins, and the idea of him being a daring raider seemed totally ridiculous.

The thought went out of his head entirely a moment later, when Zak interrupted his reverie with the news that Danny Bright had been given a three-match suspension for getting sent off. In reply, Dan told Zak about the awful chant the twins had made up about the Muddington Rovers defender.

"I wish someone would show them the red card," he muttered.

"Only not this afternoon," Zak pointed out.

"No," Dan agreed.

Then they went off to get Sam.

Chapter Eight
STINGING THE BEES

Most of the teams in the Muddington District Junior League were boys only. Leggs United were unusual in having so many girls. Belmont Bees also had girls in their team – the Mann sisters, Alice and Kate. Alice was a friend of Sam's and was coming round to tea after the match. But that was later. Now, the two were on opposing sides and each was determined to win. The two teams were level on points in the league and whoever won would go into second place.

"Good luck, Sam," Alice said before the game. "May the best team win."

"Yeah," Sam grinned. "As long as it's us."

Dan knew he was going to have his work cut out that afternoon. Alice Mann was difficult to mark. She was tall and very thin – her legs were like bamboo sticks – and she was really fast.

When the teams had played at Belmont earlier in the season, the score had been one–all and Alice had scored a brilliant goal. Some of the Belmont tackling, Dan also recalled, had been a bit fierce. At least this afternoon, he was relieved to note, they had a referee who seemed to know the rules. He called the two captains, Dan and Alice, forward for the toss and, unlike Keith Dixon, he had a coin ready. Dan won and chose to kick off.

"Come on, you Leggs!" shouted Stephen Legg heartily from the touchline. He and his sister Julia Browne, Zak's mum, were the only Leggs United parents watching that afternoon. The others were all working.

Archie was there, though, of course. He stood in his normal pose with his arms folded and one foot on the old football. He'd thoroughly enjoyed all the extra attention he'd been getting, due to Sam's project, and was feeling particularly at ease with the world. He looked as if nothing could ruffle him.

However, this appearance of cool contentment lasted barely two minutes. That's how long it took for Belmont Bees to create the game's first scoring opportunity. Kate Mann picked up a loose ball in midfield and ran forward, outstripping Jack Legg, the oldest of the triplets. She pushed the ball across to her sister, Alice, who span expertly, gaining a yard on Dan, and hit a fierce shot. The shot was on target, but Leggs United's keeper, Gabby, dived and smothered the ball.

Archie was furious with his players. His face glowed like a lit barbecue and every hair on his face and head bristled with indignation.

"*Beds* are for sleeping in, not football fields!" he rasped. "Wake yourselves up!"

His command had the desired effect. From Gabby's long kick upfield, Zak passed the ball on to his cousin Frances (another of the triplets) who burst through the Belmont defence at speed and flashed a left-footed shot just past the post.

So the pattern for the game was set. It was end-to-end stuff, first one team attacking and then the other. But it was the defences of both sides that were on top and when the referee blew for half-time the score was still nil–nil. There was nothing to choose between the two teams.

"These Bees certainly have a sting in their tail," Archie remarked when his team gathered for their half-time talk and refreshment. "Somehow, we shall have to find a way of drawing it and stinging *them* where it hurts." He peered down thoughtfully at the old ball as if searching for inspiration.

When he looked up again, his eyes were

flickering with excitement. "But that is it," he enthused. "That is *exactly* what we shall do."

"What?" Dan queried. "You want us to sting them?"

"Buzz, buzz, buzz," went Giles, waving his arms like wings.

"Zzub, zzub, zzub," Justin retorted, waving his arms too.

"Zzub, zzub, zzub?" Archie repeated questioningly.

"Yes, that's a bee flying backwards," said Justin, and he and Giles collapsed in a fit of laughter.

"Hmm, very amusing, I'm sure," Archie muttered with a disapproving wiggle of his big moustache. "But the sting I was referring to was a classic Chapman ploy. Draw your opponents on, let them think they've got you on the run, fall back before them, encourage them to throw players forward in attack . . . Then, just as they think they have you, you sting them." Archie's eyes glittered triumphantly.

The team stared at their phantom manager, waiting for some further explanation. But it wasn't Archie but Sam who spoke. "What you want," she said with a reflective wrinkle of her small nose, "are rapier-like attacks that have the spirit of adventure about them."

All eyes now turned in surprise to look at Sam.

"What did you say?" Dan enquired, pulling at one ear.

"I was just quoting Herbert Chapman," Sam answered casually. "I read it in that book this morning."

Archie beamed with pleasure. "Excellent, excellent, laddy," he purred. "I see your research is paying off already. We shall make a genius of you yet!"

Sam's grin was almost as wide as the pitch.

If Sam's research paid off, so too did Archie's sting plan. Within five minutes of the restart, Leggs United lured the Bees into over-committing themselves.

The home team pulled everyone but Zak back into defence, inviting the visitors to go forward in numbers. When the Belmont attack broke down, Leggs United flew forward. Dan found Sam and she quickly switched the ball to Zak, who raced towards the Belmont goal with Ben and Frances sprinting on either side of him.

The three Leggs attackers had only two Belmont defenders ahead of them. As one of them came to tackle Zak, he slid the ball to his right into the path of Ben, who had a clear run on goal. The keeper couldn't decide whether to come out or stay on his line and by the time he'd made up his mind to move, Ben had slipped the ball past him into the corner of the net. Leggs United were in the lead!

The goal was a good one, but Ben's celebration cartwheel wasn't. It looked more like a wheel falling *off* a cart than turning round. But

at least he didn't end up in the mud like last time.

"Great goal, Ben!" called Julia Browne.

"Yes, let's have another!" urged Stephen Legg.

Archie said nothing. He didn't need to. His smug, satisfied expression said it all.

The Belmont Bees weren't going to be stung twice, though. For the rest of the game, they played much more cautiously and were unlucky not to equalize when Alice Mann fired a cannonball shot against the bar. But in the final minute, Zak sealed the game for Leggs United with a brilliant solo goal, beating three defenders before scoring. Leggs United had won and moved into second place in the league!

On the touchline, Archie did a little victory jig, his knobbly knees pumping up and down comically.

Dan was standing there, grinning at the antics of the phantom manager, when the referee came up to him.

"Nice game, son," he said. "You hardly needed me at all."

"Thanks," Dan said happily. It was true, he realized; there had been very few fouls and the ref hadn't had to blow his whistle much – not like the previous Saturday. Remembering that, he asked, "Do you know a ref called Keith Dixon?"

The referee frowned. "Never heard of him," he shrugged. "Must be new."

"Yeah," said Dan. His eyes looked back towards the touchline where Archie was now congratulating his players. Dan started to walk towards them and Alice Mann joined him.

"Did I hear you talking about Keith Dixon?" she enquired.

"Yes," said Dan. "He's a referee. Do you know him?"

"Yeah, I know him all right," Alice replied, nodding. "He's useless. He refereed our match a couple of weeks ago." She looked across at Sam, who was standing by the fence between The Meadow and her garden, waving her friend over. "When we've got changed, I'll tell you all about it," Alice said, waving back. She smiled and shook her head. "You'll never believe it . . ."

Chapter Nine
A PAIR OF CROOKS

The tale Alice told Sam, Dan and Zak at tea that afternoon wasn't as incredible as she'd imagined. In fact to her three listeners it was all amazingly familiar. The events she described were almost exactly the same as those of the previous Saturday when Leggs United had played Old Malden – even down to the bizarre sending-off.

"Poor Harvey," Alice said sympathetically. "It was his very first match for St Luke's and he got shown the red card for doing absolutely nothing."

"Did you say Harvey?" Dan demanded excitedly.

"Yeah, Harvey," Alice replied, a little

bemused. "Why, do you know him?"

"He played against us last week," Dan explained. "For Old Malden." Then, with help from Sam and Zak, he told Alice everything that had taken place the previous Saturday.

When he got to the bit about the theft, Alice's eyes opened wide. "But that's exactly what happened in our match!" she exclaimed. "A thief went into the St Luke's changing room during the game and stole some money."

Dan's eyes narrowed thoughtfully. "Did Harvey see the thief, by any chance?"

"Yes, he did," Alice replied. "He said the man was tall and bald with shifty green eyes. And he was wearing sunglasses."

Dan frowned. "How could he see the colour of the man's eyes if he was wearing sunglasses?" he mused.

Sam humphed. "I reckon he made that up," she said with a dismissive toss of her head. "It's like that description he gave us. He said the man had a hat that was striped like a leopard!" She and Alice laughed.

"But why would he make it up?" Zak wondered earnestly.

"Well, it's obvious, isn't it?" Dan answered emphatically. "Harvey *is* the thief." He paused theatrically for an instant, before continuing, "And something else is obvious as well – Keith Dixon's in on it too."

Over the next few minutes, Dan made out his case against the hapless referee and Harvey. For a start, he said, he didn't believe Keith Dixon was a real ref. He didn't even know the rules. And why was it that Harvey kept playing for different teams? And each time he played for a new team he got sent off for nothing by Keith Dixon and then there was a robbery.

It was all too much of a coincidence. Harvey and Keith Dixon were obviously working together, Dan claimed. Keith Dixon showed Harvey the red card so that he could go back to the changing room and steal things. Then Harvey pretended he'd seen a thief so that no one would suspect him – only he wasn't a very good liar. His descriptions were ridiculous and didn't make sense.

Sam still wasn't completely convinced by Dan's accusation. "I don't know," she said, her freckly forehead wrinkling in a frown. "It seems like a lot of bother to go to just to steal a watch and some money."

"Yeah," Alice Mann agreed.

Dan nodded. "I know," he conceded. "But the thing is, I think there's more to it than that." He told the others about the report he'd read in the paper that morning at the library. He still couldn't see Keith Dixon as a warehouse raider, but maybe his job was to sell the stuff after it had been stolen.

"He's a fence," said Zak matter-of-factly.

"Eh?" said Sam, giving her cousin a quizzical stare. "More like a brick wall, I reckon."

"No, that's what they call someone who sells things that have been stolen," Zak explained.

"Oh," said Sam.

"You mean he pretends to be a ref, so that he won't seem suspicious," Alice interpreted.

"Precisely," said Dan. "And he's got lots of football-mad children to sell his stuff to." He looked pointedly at Sam.

"But what can we do about it?" Alice remarked. "We haven't got any proof."

"No," Dan sighed. "We need some real evidence." He pursed his lips grimly. "I bet we'd find some in Keith Dixon's house," he said. "But we don't even know where he lives."

"We've got his phone number," Sam declared animatedly, flicking back her fringe. "We could phone him up and ask to go round. We could say we were interested in buying a shirt or something."

Dan shook his head. "Mum and Dad would never let us go," he stated gloomily. "And anyway, how could we search the place when he was there with us?"

To the surprise of the others, Sam met Dan's objection with a broad grin. "*We* couldn't," she stressed.

"What?" Dan muttered, puzzled. "I don't . . ." And then, suddenly, he understood what his sister was getting at *and* what a brilliant idea it was. Now he smiled too. "Archie," he said softly. "We'll get Archie to help."

"Who's Archie?" asked Alice.

"Oh, he's, er . . . a friend of ours," Sam answered. "He's very good at, er . . ." Her freckly face scrunched into a frown as she floundered to find the right word.

"He's very good at helping," Dan offered.

"Yes," Sam agreed.

Later, after Alice had gone home, Sam summoned Archie from the old ball.

The phantom footballer appeared to be a little pale and woozy at first, but after fixing his gaze on the TV for a few seconds, he was back to his normal shimmering self.

"Now," he boomed. "To what do I owe this pleasure?"

As the children explained the situation to him, Archie listened with great interest and attention, almost as if he were being told some fascinating new development in football tactics. When asked to help, he was only too happy to oblige.

"I knew there was something awry with that referee fellow," he intoned gravely with a twitch of his moustache. "He had a criminal's eyes."

"A criminal's eyes?" Zak queried. "What are they?"

"Well, you know," Archie muttered vaguely. "Sort of small and shifty and always on the lookout for cake."

"Cake?" Sam repeated.

"Yes, cake," said Archie. "Criminals love cake – especially other people's."

Dan stared at his ghostly ancestor with a

bewildered expression. "I don't know what on earth you're on about, Archie," he said at last.

"Ah well," Archie sighed. "It is the fate of genius to be misunderstood."

The three children looked at each other and sighed.

Chapter Ten
ARCHIE PLAYS DETECTIVE

Next day, the plan was set in motion. Sam phoned up Keith Dixon and got his address. She said she wanted to go round later with her dad to buy a couple of football shirts.

"Any time, son, any time," wheezed the ref cordially. "I'll be here."

"Yes, but I won't," Sam thought, as she hung up the receiver. Then she and Dan called up Archie and sent him on his way.

The following hours, while they waited for his return, seemed to last for ever.

"Is he back yet?" Zak asked eagerly when he came round after lunch.

But Sam shook her head. "There's still no sign of him," she said.

To pass the time, Dan, Sam and Zak went down to the Meadow to have a kick-about.

It was an hour or so before they came back to the house and when they looked in the sitting room, Archie was there. He was hovering by the table, flicking through Sam's project.

"There is no 'e' in Highbury," he remarked critically to Sam, as the children joined him.

"Never mind that!" Sam cried. "How did you get on? What did you find out?"

Archie's moustache waggled smugly. "I have uncovered the whole sordid business," he proclaimed. He gestured to the chairs around the table. "Sit down and all shall be revealed," he said grandly.

Dan's suspicions about Keith Dixon had been spot on, Archie confirmed. He was indeed a member of the gang that had been raiding sports warehouses – in fact, he was the leader! Archie had heard it all from the lips of the crooked ref himself, speaking on the telephone to another member of the gang. As Dan had suggested, Keith Dixon didn't actually take part in the raids, but he planned them and then he sold the stolen goods afterwards. His house was full of the stuff.

"I discovered something else most interesting too," Archie continued. "While I was in that thief's den, he had a visitor." Archie paused dramatically.

"Who was it?" Dan prompted.

"The visitor," Archie went on, "was none other than that lad who was shown the red card by our ref."

"Harvey!" Dan exclaimed.

"So they *do* know each other," Zak concluded.

"Know each other?" Archie repeated. "I should think they do!" He raised one bushy eyebrow. "Keith Dixon is Harvey's uncle," the phantom manager revealed, to the children's amazement. "And they're planning another of their criminal capers this Saturday at Marchmont," Archie continued. "Harvey will be playing for their opponents, Thornley Diamonds."

"He's playing for another team!" Dan exclaimed. "He changes teams more often than Herbert Chapman!"

"The more teams he plays for, the more he can

rob," Archie stated with a disgusted wrinkle of his big moustache. "Talking of which . . ." He waved a bony hand towards the glass cabinet, where the old ball was kept. On top, next to an old photo of the ghostly footballer himself, was a fancy gold watch. "I took the liberty of retrieving some stolen property," he said nonchalantly.

Dan realized at once whose watch it was. "It's Ash's dad's watch, isn't it?" he said, impressed. "You got it back."

"Cool," uttered Zak appreciatively.

"You're a genius, Archie," Sam affirmed.

Archie shrugged. "Tell me something new."

As well as finding out all this information, Archie now revealed, he'd also had a bit of fun at the crooked ref's expense. He'd emptied out the clothes from his wardrobe and chucked his pants and socks out of the bedroom window into the street below. One pair of pants had wrapped itself around the head of a passing dog while another, with a bright tartan pattern, had impaled itself on a fence post, where it had flapped in the wind like a flag.

All in all, everyone agreed, Archie's detective mission had been a spectacular success. He had

even found out the time and place arranged for the gang's next warehouse raid. It was to take place that Friday night.

"We ought to tell the police," said Sam.

"Yeah," agreed Zak.

"But what if they don't believe us?" Dan quibbled with a tug at one ear. "I mean, we're just kids, aren't we? They probably won't take us seriously."

"Well, get Dad to phone," Sam suggested.

Dan looked troubled. "I don't know if that's a good idea," he said. "Supposing they ask him how he knew. He can't say a ghost told him, can he? They'd think he was crazy."

"You mean they do not believe in ghosts?" Archie questioned, his eyes all a-fizz.

"Of course not," Sam snorted. "Nobody does." She stopped suddenly, spotting the look of outrage in her ancient relative's eyes. "Well, apart from us, of course," she added quickly. "We *know* ghosts exist."

"Yes," Dan nodded. "But the police don't." He didn't look disheartened, though. "It's OK, though, cos I've had another idea," he said. "*I'll* phone the police and tip them off about the raid."

"But they'll just think you're a boy, messing about," Sam objected.

"Precisely," agreed Archie.

"No, I'll disguise my voice," Dan retorted, "so that I sound like a man. Listen." He pulled his shirt up over his mouth and, in a funny sort-of-croaky voice, said, "There's going to be a raid at Bob's Sporting Emporium this Friday evening."

Sam and Zak sniggered.

"You sound weird," Sam laughed.

"Yeah," agreed Zak.

"It doesn't matter," Dan muttered testily. "As long as they get the information."

Archie yawned. "It's time I retired to my pig's bladder," he murmured wearily. "All this detective work has quite exhausted me. Now I know why Sherlock Holmes spent so much of his time sitting in an armchair playing the violin." He yawned again. "You have heard of Sherlock Holmes, I take it?" he enquired.

"Yes, of course," said Sam, as her phantom relative disappeared into the old ball. Then, when he'd vanished completely, she added cheekily, "He played in goal for West Ham, didn't he?"

Dan and Zak laughed. But a moment later Dan's face took on a determined expression.

"Right," he said grimly. "Now, let's get on with the serious business."

Chapter Eleven
ARCHIE BLOWS THE WHISTLE

On Saturday morning, Dan and Sam heard on the local radio station that the police had arrested three men in the act of robbing Bob's Sporting Emporium. The men were suspected of being behind a number of other similar raids in the area, the reporter continued.

Leggs United didn't have a match that Saturday, so Dan, Sam and Zak decided to cycle to Marchmont, whose ground was only a couple of miles away. Sam carried the old ball in a basket at the front of her bike.

It was Harvey they saw first. This time he was in the strip of Thornley Diamonds, Marchmont's opponents that afternoon. He looked a little uneasy when he saw the Leggs players.

"I see you've joined another team," Dan remarked pleasantly.

"Oh, yeah," said Harvey uncomfortably. "I didn't really like Old Malden."

"What about St Luke's?" Sam commented casually.

Harvey blushed. He looked like a rabbit caught in a trap. "Er, well, no," he muttered. "I just helped them out for one game, you know." Then he quickly scuttled away to join his latest team-mates.

Keith Dixon was a little taken aback as well to see the Leggs United players.

"Oh, hello, kids," he wheezed, his many chins wobbling. "What brings you here today?"

"We thought we'd come and check out Marchmont," Dan said airily. "We've got to play them soon in the league."

"Oh, I see," said Keith Dixon and he smiled amiably. "Eyeing up the opposition, eh? Very wise."

Sam stepped forward. "Sorry I didn't come round last Sunday," she apologized. "Maybe I could look at those shirts again after the match. I've got some money." She didn't add that this money amounted to precisely 27 pence.

Keith Dixon raised his hands in a gesture of happy generosity. "Of course," he said. His little eyes gazed greedily at the old ball in Zak's hands as if it were a large chocolate pudding. "You could put your ball in my room if you like, while the match is on," he offered. "It'll be safe there."

"OK, thanks," said Dan. Then he winced as Sam gave him a sharp kick on the ankle.

"What was that for?" Dan asked ruefully, when Keith Dixon had waddled away towards the pitch.

"I'm not putting our ball in that thief's room," Sam declared fiercely. "Harvey'll steal it."

Dan shook his head and sighed. "Of course he will," he said pityingly.

"Eh?" said Sam quizzically. "You want Harvey to steal our ball?"

"Yes," said Dan. "Then we can catch him red-handed." He beamed proudly. "Good idea, don't you think? It just came to me."

"Yeah, cool," Zak nodded.

Sam looked at the two boys with a bemused

expression. "Would someone like to tell me what's going on?" she demanded sharply.

"Call up Archie," Dan commanded, "and then I'll explain."

Dan's idea was simple enough. They knew Keith Dixon thought the old ball was valuable, so they'd use it as bait to trap him and Harvey. While Sam and Dan watched the game, Archie would stay with the ball and Zak would wait by the telephone kiosk. When the ref sent off his nephew, Zak would phone the police.

"Do you think they'll get here in time?" asked Sam doubtfully.

Dan frowned. "Good point," he said. He turned to his phantom relative. "Archie, you'll have to stall Harvey until the police arrive," he instructed.

"Leave it to Archibald Legg," Archie proclaimed, tapping a bony finger to his nose. "Those swindlers won't know what's hit them." His big moustache bristled and his eyebrows formed a fiery V. "There's nothing so rewarding as seeing foul play get its just deserts," he growled.

Keith Dixon's performance was as bizarre as ever. He awarded free-kicks for non-existent fouls, failed to penalize obvious infringements and still didn't seem to know what sport he was refereeing. At one point Dan was sure he heard him shout "Touch-down!" as though the teams were playing American football!

Harvey, meanwhile, started with more spirit than he'd shown against Leggs United, but after Marchmont took the lead he quickly appeared to lose interest. Twenty minutes from the end of the match, as Dan had expected, Keith Dixon produced his red card and, for no apparent reason, waved it at his nephew.

"This is it," Dan whispered excitedly to Sam. Then he turned and waved to Zak. Their plan was up and running!

The next minutes passed agonizingly slowly for Sam and Dan, standing by the pitch, waiting to find out whether their plan had been successful. They were dying to run back to the changing rooms and see if Harvey had taken the bait, but they knew they had to hang on until the police appeared. If they disturbed Harvey now, then he'd be away by the time the police arrived and the plan would be ruined.

The minutes passed. Finally, with the game

almost over, a siren sounded. Moments later, a police car turned in to the park. Dan and Sam sighed with relief. Zak's phone call had done the trick. But had Archie managed to delay Harvey?

"You stay here and keep an eye on the ref. I'll go and help Zak and Archie," Dan breathed. Then, before Sam could protest, he sprinted away towards the changing rooms.

He arrived just as Harvey appeared from round the back of the building. His face was white as snow and his eyes were bulging with terror. An instant later, Dan understood why. Archie was pursuing Harvey with the old ball in his hands.

"Help!" squeaked Harvey. "The ball's after me!"

Dan grinned. Harvey couldn't see Archie, only the ball, so he thought it was moving through the air on its own: a demon ball!

Archie strolled up to the now-frozen Harvey and, nonchalantly, placed the ball in his trembling hands. Harvey looked at it in horror. It was in this pose that the two policemen found him moments later when they marched onto the scene accompanied by Zak.

"That's him," said Zak, pointing at Harvey. "That's the thief."

"He stole our ball from the changing room," Dan added. Then, gesturing towards Harvey's pockets, he continued, "He's taken money too. He's done it before."

Quickly, Dan informed the policemen of the previous thefts and how they had been perpetrated. "He and the ref are in it together," he concluded. Then, dramatically, he announced, "The ref's his uncle."

Harvey's look of horror turned to astonishment.

"How do you know that?" he gasped.

Dan glanced at Archie who was standing next to Harvey, beaming.

"We did some detective work," he said matter-of-factly. "We know all about you and your uncle."

A whistle peeped shrilly three times.

"Where is this uncle, then?" asked one of the policemen.

"He's over there refereeing and he's just blown the final whistle," Dan replied.

"His name's Keith Dixon," Zak chipped in.

At the mention of the ref's name, the two policemen did a double-take.

"We're looking for him," said one excitedly. "We've just been told he's part of a gang stealing sports equipment."

"We caught the rest of the gang last night," said the other policeman.

"Yeah, we heard about it on the news," Dan confirmed.

"Right," said the first policeman to his colleague. "You hold on to this one" – he nodded at Harvey – "and I'll go and get Dixon."

Dan and Zak ran on ahead of the policeman,

but it was Archie who moved the fastest. He glided above the grass at an amazing pace.

Keith Dixon was still on the pitch when the phantom manager reached him. Archie rose up impressively before him. "Scoundrel, knave, cheat!" he exclaimed. He pulled the red card from the ref's top pocket and flourished it in front of his flabbergasted face. Then he leant forward and blew a loud blast on the ref's whistle.

Keith Dixon's little eyes almost popped out of his head.

"A-a-a," he stammered. His face quivered like a big white blancmange, as he stared at the red card and whistle, seemingly floating in the air before him.

"For you, sir," Archie declaimed, pointing one bony finger towards the approaching policeman, "the game is up!"

Chapter Twelve
A GHOSTLY ENDING

"You should have seen Harvey's face," Dan laughed. "He really did look like he'd seen a ghost."

"I gave him a bit of a scare, that's for sure," Archie snorted with a broad smile of his own.

They were in the sitting room, reliving for the umpteenth time the success of their afternoon at Marchmont several days before.

"There he was, hiding the ball in the bushes," Archie went on, "planning no doubt to return and retrieve it later, when out it popped again in the arms of yours truly. I have never seen such awful dread on a face in all my life – or my death either." He drew himself up haughtily. "No one steals Archibald Legg's ball and gets away with it," he declared dramatically.

The door flew open and in rushed Sam, clutching a notebook. Her freckly face was animated with delight and excitement. Behind her entered the caterwauling noise of the twins singing their Danny Bright chant. Sam quickly pushed the door shut.

"Hey, Archie, guess what?" she cried. "Mrs Waters said my project was the best in the whole class." She clutched the notebook to her chest ecstatically.

Archie's face glowed with proud satisfaction. "Naturally," he murmured. "You had the help of genius."

Sam and Dan looked at each other and rolled their eyes.

"She particularly liked the ending," Sam went on. "And that bit didn't have anything to do with you. I got it from that book at the library."

"Well, of course, books have their place in such matters," Archie carped, with a wiggle of his walrus moustache. "But you cannot beat the opinion of one who was actually there."

"But you weren't there, Archie, that's the point," Sam insisted.

Archie regarded his young relative with a bewildered frown. "Whatever do you mean, laddy?" he demanded.

"Well, you were, er, dead – and so was Herbert Chapman," Sam explained. "But he came back as a ghost too."

"Herbert Chapman, a ghost?" Archie queried.

"Yes," said Sam. She opened the notebook at the end and, in a theatrical voice, she declaimed, "*For several years after the great manager's death, his*

ghostly footsteps were heard, striding through the corridors of Highbury." She stopped and grinned. "A good ending, don't you think?" she chirped, laying the notebook on the table in front of Archie.

The phantom footballer nodded his big head appreciatively. "Not bad," he conceded, "not bad at all." He glanced at the book in front of him. Then, raising one red caterpillar eyebrow, he added sharply, "But there's still no 'e' in Highbury."

Leggs United 6
TEAM ON TOUR

Leggs United are away on tour, staying in a creepy old castle. But scary noises in the night keep the team awake, making them play their worst match ever . . .

Can Archie their phantom manager sort out the troublesome spook – and get his team back on the ball?

"Laugh yourself into another league."
Young Telegraph

Collect all the **Leggs United** books!

The prices shown below are correct at the time of going to press.
However, Macmillan Publishers reserve the right to show new
retail prices on covers which may differ from those previously
advertised.

All Macmillan titles can be ordered at your local bookshop
or are available by post from:

**Book Service by Post
PO Box 29, Douglas, Isle of Man IM99 1BQ**

Credit cards accepted. For details:
Telephone: 01624 675137
Fax: 01624 670923
E-mail: bookshop@enterprise.net

Free postage and packing in the UK.
Overseas customers: add £1 per book (paperback)
and £3 per book (hardback).